PUMPKIN PIE

Written by Harriet Ziefert

Pumpkin Pie

Paintings by Donald Dreifuss

HOUGHTON MIFFLIN COMPANY BOSTON

Walter Lorraine Books

For Mimi,
who puts up with it all
—D.D.

Walter Lorraine *wr* Books

Text copyright © 2000 by Harriet Ziefert
Illustrations copyright © 2000 by Donald Dreifuss

Library of Congress Cataloging-in-Publication Data

Ziefert, Harriet.
    Pumpkin Pie / by Harriet Ziefert ; illustrated by Donald Dreifuss.
        p.cm.
    Summary: Pumpkin Pie the goat enters a competition at the fair.
Includes information on the life cycle, physical characteristics, and
behavior of dairy goats.
    ISBN 0-618-04883-9
        [1. Goats—Fiction] I. Dreifuss, Donald, ill. II. Title.
        PZ7.Z487 Mr 2000
        [E]—dc21

                                        99-042850
                                        CIP

Printed in China for Harriet Ziefert, Inc.
HZI 10 9 8 7 6 5 4 3 2 1

My real name is Pumpkin Pie. But everyone calls me Pumpkin. I live on Britton Hill Farm with one hundred other goats. But I am the favorite!

I am the one Donald picks for the big
Fourth of July show in Unity.

Donald will take me there to see if
I can win a blue ribbon for our farm.

Sometimes I get into trouble.

Goat trouble . . .

garbage trouble . . .

fence trouble! But when it happens,
Donald doesn't get too mad. Lucky me!

Donald wants to clip me and trim my feet before the show. I DO NOT like clipping.

I DO NOT like trimming.

And I DO NOT like baths!

Yesterday I stuffed myself. Today I have a bad stomach ache, which is serious when you have four stomachs!

Donald says, "Don't be scared, Pumpkin.
Dr. Max is a good veterinarian."

Donald wants me to get better fast, so he
feeds me special mush for a few days.

Now we're off to the fair.
Wish us luck.

Here we are at the fairgrounds.
I see many other goat farmers.

And so many goats!

We have to wait our turn.
"Steady, Pumpkin," says Donald. "Be still."

But I don't like being still. The judges
push and poke and inspect me.

I DO NOT like being inspected!
I don't mean to kick the judge.

But I do! And I'm sorry.

Donald and I do not win a ribbon.

But we come close.

"Maybe next year," says Donald.

"Meh . . . meh . . . meh . . . ," I answer.

Farmer Donald takes care of:

50 nubian goats

25 saanen goats

50 Jacob's four-horned sheep

2 cows

1 large tree frog

7 parrots

2 whippets

1 donkey

100 assorted chickens

4 emu

8 peacocks

1 iguana

5 pigs

1 colony of parakeets

2 beehives

10 Muscovy ducks

8 Toulouse geese

3 blue-eyed Embden geese

Farmer Donald speaks:

The dairy goats in this story are Nubian and Toggenburg. They are bred for milk production and are slim and bony. Pumpkin Pie is a 3-year-old Toggenburg.

Size:
Dairy goats weigh between 135 and 160 pounds. They are approximately four feet tall.

Growing Up:
Baby goats grow up quickly and are ready to give milk and have babies of their own after one year. Dairy goats live for about 12 years.

Food:
Dairy goats like to eat rough plant materials, especially brambles and fruit trees. I feed them hay, alfalfa, timothy, and legumes. If a goat eats too much green grass, or too much grain, it will become bloated and sick, just like Pumpkin Pie.

Milking:

A dairy goat's udders have two teats and hold a lot of milk. The milk is sweet and delicious to drink, and it also can be used to make cheese. Dairy goats need to be milked every twelve hours (twice a day). My best goats give two gallons of milk a day.

Clipping:

All goats are clipped to the skin in the spring. If a goat is going to be in a show, her fur is clipped a week before. Goats have fast-growing, cloven hoofs. Their hoofs need trimming every 3 or 4 weeks.

Baths:

Goats are clean animals and don't usually need baths. However, before a show a goat is given special treatment—a bath with baby shampoo and shine to polish her hoofs and coat.

Sounds:

A Nubian goat is loud.
It bleats sound like:
maa...maa...blahhh!
A Toggenburg goat is not as noisy.
The bleats are softer and sweeter:
meh...meh...meh...